Redline

Redline

Alex Van Tol

orca soundings

ORCA BOOK PUBLISHERS

Library and Archives Canada Cataloguing in Publication

Van Tol, Alex
Redline / Alex Van Tol.
(Orca soundings)

Issued also in electronic format.
ISBN 978-1-55469-894-3 (bound).--ISBN 978-1-55469-893-6 (pbk.)

I. Title. II. Series: Orca soundings
PS8643.A63R43 2011   JC813'.6   C2011-903430-1

First published in the United States, 2011
Library of Congress Control Number: 2011929394

Summary: Jenessa uses the thrill of illegal street racing to deal with
the tragic death of her best friend.

*Orca Book Publishers is dedicated to preserving the environment and has printed
this book on paper certified by the Forest Stewardship Council®.*

Orca Book Publishers gratefully acknowledges the support for its publishing
programs provided by the following agencies: the Government of Canada
through the Canada Book Fund and the Canada Council for the Arts,
and the Province of British Columbia through the BC Arts Council
and the Book Publishing Tax Credit.

Cover photography by Getty Images

ORCA BOOK PUBLISHERS
PO Box 5626, Stn. B
Victoria, BC Canada
V8R 6S4

ORCA BOOK PUBLISHERS
PO Box 468
Custer, WA USA
98240-0468

www.orcabook.com
Printed and bound in Canada.

14 13 12 11 • 4 3 2 1

For Mum and Dad, who watched me crash my cars...and trusted me enough to keep giving me the keys to theirs.

Chapter One

Time for a change.

I spin my thumb around on my iPod, looking for a different playlist. I glance up at the road, then back down. The highway is quiet tonight. Must be because it's a Monday. Everyone's back in town. Back from a weekend in the mountains, getting those last few runs in before the hills close down for the spring.

I used to like driving west, toward the mountains. Sometimes, if I was out late enough after work, I would see the aurora borealis. The northern lights. Usually they're just a green fringe moving slowly across the sky. This one time they were a brilliant, crazy violet.

No matter the color, they always take my breath away.

But tonight, instead of heading west, I point my car south, toward McCandless Creek. The mountains hold too many painful memories.

I drive through ranch country. Sometimes I take the hilly back roads through the huge, barn-studded acreages.

Sometimes.

Usually I just take it out the six-lane and punch it. It helps me outrun the pain.

I reach for a cigarette, then pause. Maybe not. Maybe that's one thing

I should let go of. I punish my mind enough by reliving that awful day on Mount Watson. I don't need to punish my body too.

Without my permission, my mind drifts back. To a day that will forever be burned into my brain. Every detail of it.

It was November, just before midterms. Adrienne and I had been about to wrap a primo day of boarding. The sun was out. Conditions had been perfect. We'd been chatted up by some sweet boys in the lift lineup and had plans to meet up with them later, back at the resort.

It was almost four o'clock. Ade was tired. I could see that. I was too.

We'd just come off what we had agreed would be our last run of the day. Swooping to a stop at the end of the lift line, I glanced at the clock over the lodge. Still enough time. If we went now, we could catch just *one* more run.

I was feeling pretty flush, ready for another crack at the Terminator 2. A triple black diamond. I'd smoke it this time. I was sure of it.

But Adrienne hadn't wanted to. She was cold and hungry, and she wanted to go in.

"Just one more, Ade," I said, hoping the energy in my voice would somehow flow into her and make this possible. "Let's run T2."

The look on her face told me she didn't want to do it.

"Come on," I said as she started to shake her head. "You did it this morning. You killed it!"

Adrienne snorted. "I *so* didn't kill it, Jenessa. It almost killed *me*."

I shrugged. "You'll ride it better this time. You've already done it. Your brain's mapped it now."

Adrienne sighed. "I don't know." She squinted at the sun, low on the peaks.

4

"Don't they say that ski accidents increase by something like two hundred percent in the late afternoon? When people are tired?"

I bent down to fiddle with my binding, pissed that she was holding out on me. "You go on in then," I said. "I'll catch up with you in a few." I knew I was laying on the guilt.

"You can't go up there alone, Ness," she said. "What if you get hurt?"

I stood up and leveled my gaze at her. "You forget, my friend," I said. "*I* don't get hurt. *Lesser* boarders get hurt." I tucked an escaped strand of hair back under my helmet. "I'm no lightweight," I added. I couldn't help myself.

So she came.

How could she not? I'd thrown down the gauntlet, daring her not to join me. I'd done it so many times before with Adrienne. And she always pulled it out for me. Taking that one step outside her comfort zone. To keep the peace.

We caught the lift up, our chair bobbing on the wire, high over the quickly emptying hill. The patrols were getting ready to do their sweep runs. Ade was jittery. "Don't worry," I told her. "I got your back."

We were halfway down the Terminator when an out-of-control skier smashed into Adrienne.

She was ahead of me. I saw the whole thing. His scarecrow scramble as he tried to avoid her. Her helmet whiplashing backward on impact. Her board, sliced clean off its leash, bolting down the hill. Her body, thrown into the spruce tree at the side of the run. Her neck bending impossibly.

Lesser boarders get hurt.

The redness of the snow as I held her in my arms and screamed for help.

I'm no lightweight.

The blueness of her eyes as she looked at me, confused.

I got your back.

The blackness of my heart, knowing I had just killed my best friend.

The memory runs its course. It leaves me slowly, like a cold blade being eased out of my chest. My teeth are hurting, and I try to unclench my jaw. My knuckles are white on the steering wheel.

I press my foot to the floor, my eyes unblinking as I watch the speedometer climb. Seventy miles an hour. Eighty. Ninety. A hundred.

One twenty. The engine roars its pleasure. The needle climbs.

I crack my window and spark up a smoke. What the hell.

Tonight's a good night to die.

Chapter Two

But I don't.

Three hours later, I pull into the driveway of my dad's new house, deep in the suburbs of our city. I'm exhausted, spent, shaking.

Adrienne died six months ago. Half a year. But in my mind, it feels like yesterday.

Ade was my only real friend. I never considered that I might ever need more friends than her. I don't have anyone else. I didn't think I needed anyone else.

I lift my chin. I *don't* need anyone else. Dad's right when he says we're all alone in this world. It's best to figure out how to be on your own. Not depend on other people for things. For favors. For friendship. For love.

Back when Adrienne moved onto our block, I had tried to keep to myself. But she just wouldn't give up. She saw something in me that she liked, I guess. I was twelve at the time. She just kept dropping by the house to talk. I got tired of trying to push her away. So I let her in. I let her like me. And I let myself like her.

Which I should never have done, because look how it turned out for her.

And look how it turned out for me.

God, look how it turned out for my dad. Fifteen years of marriage, a ten-year-old kid, and boom: Mom just up and leaves.

I don't need anyone else. I don't *want* anyone else. It just complicates things. Because as soon as you let someone in, you're done. You're not standing on your own anymore.

I went to my mom's place over Christmas break, shortly after Ade's death. I spend my vacations with her at her place in Palm Springs. It was good to go away this time. I needed to put some distance between me and what had happened. Between me and all the whispers that erupted as soon as I'd pass people in the hallway at school.

At first, Mom tried to help me sort through some stuff. But in the end, she just gave me space. It was all I could handle.

When I came back in January, I started looking for a car. You would think that as the only child of an oil baron, I'd have gotten a free ride. That my father would have just bought me a car with the wads of money he's got lying around. But there's no sugar coming from this daddy. He grew up in a regular family. He says hard work got him to where he is now. Calls himself a self-made man. And no self-made man is going to buy his kid a car if he knows that she can do it herself. He's all about self-reliance. He "sees the value" in making me work for what I want. Or something like that.

Obviously, I don't see quite as much value in it. But arguing with my dad over money is like bashing your head against a brick wall. It doesn't get you anywhere, and at the end of it, all you're left with is a headache.

I'd been saving for two years for my car, working at the tutoring agency. I help kids with their math. I'm no nerd: it's grade-five stuff. Anybody could do it. And the money is pretty good. There's not much else a person my age can do that brings in $25 an hour. Not much that's legal anyway.

I knew I wanted a Mustang GT. My dad and I looked on the AutoTrader website until I found the perfect one last week. Low mileage. Recent year. A nice loud yellow.

Va*room*.

Dad offered to come with me to help me buy it. "Close the deal" were his words, I think.

I said thanks, but no thanks. Standing on my own two feet and all.

A few days ago I went to meet the guy who was selling the car. Dmitri. He had beautiful eyes. He was handling the sale for his older brother, who was away on a navy mission in Somalia, where all those pirates have been hijacking cargo ships.

We took the car for a test drive. I was totally well-behaved behind the wheel. I wanted him to see that his brother's baby was going to a good home.

Dmitri and I talked for a long time. Mostly about cars and pirates, but also about our jobs and school and stuff like that. He goes to Geoffrey Marshall. It's pretty close to my school, Margaret May. But Marshall's a lot bigger. And their teams always kick our teams' asses, so nobody talks them up too much.

I could see the car was in amazing shape. I bartered him down by a thousand anyway. I think he was surprised.

I surprised myself by holding it together under that gaze of his.

As I drove away, I glanced in my rearview. He was standing in the middle of the road, watching me.

My phone pinged five minutes later, while I was making a left onto Leach. I grabbed it—forget those stupid new laws—and keyed in my password.

My stomach performed a full front flip.

It was a text from Dmitri. How…? Then I remembered. I'd put my contact information on the bill of sale.

My thumb hovered over the Reply option. But in the end, I didn't answer him.

There's no point. There's nothing left of my heart. Nothing left to give. Nothing left to receive.

Nothing left to break.

I've got 260 "horses under the hood," as car freaks would say.

But I'm not a car freak. I don't care about its torque or its compression ratio or even its fuel economy. I just care that it's fast as a lighting bolt, and can carry me away from my living nightmare for even just a little bit.

Dad took the car out for a test drive when I brought it home. He was clearly impressed. When he handed me the keys—like it was actually his car, as if he had anything to do with it—he made me promise I'd drive responsibly. I swore up and down that I would.

I wasn't so much lying as I was screening him from the full facts. Just like the times I'd taken his Audi out on the freeway when he was sleeping off a boozy night with the fat cats downtown at the Ranchmen's Club.

But now that I've got my own car, I don't have to steal Dad's keys. I can keep it on the up. Makes me feel a bit better about myself.

For a second or two.

I kill the engine and sit in the driveway for a few minutes, looking at the darkened house. The thought of going inside, of washing my face, brushing my teeth and climbing into bed makes me even more tired. Briefly, I consider putting my seat back and just bagging out here. Dad wouldn't even notice I was gone. But it's cold, and I guess I'd rather spend the night in my bed.

Maybe, if I'm lucky, I won't dream about Ade's accident tonight.

Chapter Three

I dream about Dmitri instead. It's a good dream. I wouldn't mind having it again. And again.

I wait for my breathing to return to normal, then open my eyes slowly. The bright sunlight of early spring fills my bedroom, making the walls yellower than they really are. My eyes fall on a photo of me and Adrienne.

We're standing in the doorway of the Palm Springs gondola. I remember that afternoon. How Ade and my mom were freaking out as I bounced the tramcar around, trying to see how much I could make it move as we rode over Chino Canyon. How my mom jumped out as soon as we slowed down, turning around to catch a photo of Ade and me as we crawled over each other to get out.

I turn my eyes away. The pleasure of my dream dissolves.

Shitty. I thought it might have been a good day.

"Small coffee, please," I say. I push a handful of change across the counter toward the tattooed, pierced barista.

Coffee dude nods and counts the coins, his dreadlocks swinging in time to the music drifting through the speakers above us. I count nine earrings jammed into a single hole in his ear. I wonder if that hurts.

"Medium roast?"

"Dark," I say. "Thanks."

"Nah. Go medium," says a familiar voice. I turn to see Dmitri grinning at me. He shrugs. "The lighter the roast, the more caffeine." His eyes are even darker than I remembered. And they're fixed on mine. Intently. I think of my dream from this morning. Suddenly I feel hot.

My tummy does a little rollercoaster thing under his gaze. I hope he can't read minds.

But then I realize if he could, we sure as hell wouldn't be standing here making conversation about coffee.

The barista pauses, watching me with one eyebrow cocked. I realize he's waiting to see whether I'm going to change my mind about my coffee.

"Dark is fine," I say. He nods again and drops my money into the change drawer. I flip a quarter into the mug where they collect tips. I turn back to Dmitri.

"Actually, I usually drink Americanos," I say. "And you? Triple-shot espressos?"

He laughs. The sound is warm, and it travels through my body, making my fingertips tingle. I can't help but look at his mouth, which was a key part of my dream.

"No triple-shot espressos for me," he says. "Not after dinner anyway. Keeps me up."

My mind grabs on to his last words, making them into something he probably didn't intend. I suspect there are things besides coffee that would keep him up. I smile a little.

"What?" he says, watching me.

My smile vanishes, and I blink. "Uh, nothing," I stumble. "It's just…" I make a show of looking at the clock behind the bar. "It's just that it's only, like, nine o'clock. On a Friday night. Are you going to bed soon?" Jesus, I'm not having much luck steering this conversation out of the innuendo zone.

"Not for a while," he says. "Plenty of night left." He smiles again. My stomach goes all funny. I'm not sure I should give it coffee right now.

"But you can't drink coffee," I say.

"Well, lives depend on me. I can't be tired when I show up to work on Saturday morning."

I raise my eyebrows. "Lives depend on you? What are you, a firefighter or something?"

He laughs again. "No. I'm a lifeguard. At Irvine. Friday nights and weekend mornings." He nods his head in the direction of the rec center. I'm surprised I haven't seen him there before. I take my little cousins swimming there sometimes. Then again, it's not like I have much time to look around me when I'm trying to keep an eye on two preschoolers.

It takes me a second to realize I've fixated on his lips again. He must think I'm crazy. Or a really bad conversationalist. "Cool," I say, pulling my eyes up to meet his. "Yeah, Irvine's, like, just up the road."

Good one, Jenessa. You're a small-talk superstar.

I try again. "I work next door. At Campbell Learning Centre. I tutor kids in math."

"So, this is your after-work party joint?" he asks, motioning around us.

"The only one."

"And what else do you do for kicks, besides order dark-roast coffee when you'd really rather have an Americano?" His words are teasing, but there's a smile in his eyes.

Without warning, that last day of snowboarding wells up in my mind.

What do I do for kicks? My throat tightens and I bite my lip. I feel tears welling up. What the hell?

I swallow down on them, hard. I turn away, picking up the hot cup of coffee that Dreads has set down on the counter for me.

"Um," I say. I step to the side so Dmitri can place his order. I take a deep breath and shove the sudden sadness away.

Dmitri meets the barista's eyes with a smile as he takes his change. He smiles a lot. And it's so friendly. "Thanks," he says to the guy. He turns to me again. "So? In your free time, you…?"

"In my free time?" I repeat. "I, uh, I…I drive," I stammer. Wow, that sounds lame. I drive?

Dmitri studies me. "You drive." Then he nods. "That makes sense," he says. "You *did* buy a flashy yellow

Mustang from me not too long ago." The corners of his mouth turn up.

I find myself staring at him again. What's going on, Jenessa? Get a grip, girl. He picks up his coffee and takes a step toward me. Like a frightened rabbit, I dart backward toward the little stand that holds the sugar and napkins. I'm not ready for this. Not prepared to have someone actually look me in the eye and treat me like a human being instead of a murderer.

But then I remember.

Dmitri's only being friendly because he doesn't know. As soon as he finds out what I did to Adrienne, the party's over.

He follows me to the coffee counter and helps himself to a lid. He presses it down around the lip of his cup, watching me. I realize he's waiting for me to say something.

"Yeah, the flashy yellow Mustang," I stammer. "It's parked right outside."

I gesture toward the door, as if he might need help locating the parking lot.

"I know. I saw it when I was driving by," he says. "Figured I'd come in and see if you were here."

I nod like this makes sense. But I can't say anything. Why does he want to see me? I look for a way to close out, to finish the conversation. It's nice enough to think about Dmitri. Maybe even dream a bit about him. But I don't want to spend any time with him. I can't afford to care.

I feel myself tightening up. The walls of the coffee shop start to press in. I fight the panic that rises in my chest.

Suddenly a blast of cool air hits my face. I can breathe again. Dmitri's holding the door open for me, a smile on his lips.

"Come on," he says. "I'll show you *my* car."

Chapter Four

A car. Okay, a car. I can handle that. It gets me out of the coffee shop. I'll go see his car. I like cars.

And then I'm calling it a night. Dmitri can go his way, and I can go mine. This will be our last meeting. My life doesn't need any more complications, thanks.

We step out into the quiet parking lot. All my dark thoughts vanish when I lay eyes on his machine. It's black, with a shiny vent-like thing mounted on the hood. White racing stripes travel the length of the car, from the hood to the tail. Every inch of chrome sparkles in the light thrown down by the streetlights. It takes my breath away.

Dmitri watches as I walk around it wordlessly, taking it all in. Flawless paint, tinted windows. Shiny chrome dual exhaust. This bugger must be *loud*.

When I've completed my circle, he grins. "You like it?"

I glance at him, then back at the car. "I do like it," I say. "What is it?" I have to ask. The model name isn't on the back. And somehow, with Dmitri, asking a stupid question seems okay.

"It's a '69 Camaro. I bought it off a guy last year and fixed it up. I've added some stuff, like the air intake," he says, nodding at the thing on the hood.

"How fast?" I ask. To me, that's all that matters.

"Five hundred horses," he says. "Top end?" He shrugs. "I don't know. I've never taken it all the way up."

Five hundred horsepower? Holy shit. My car's a Tonka truck in comparison.

I point at the intake. "How do you see around that? Is it even legal?"

Dmitri shrugs and smiles a little.

"What do you do when you get pulled over?" I ask.

"Pay the fine," he says. "I'm not a jerk about it. It's only happened once. This isn't my regular car," he adds. "Usually I walk or skate. Sometimes I take my dad's Volvo. I don't drive this thing much unless I'm out at the track."

"You race this thing at the track? What's that like?" I can't help myself.

I had no idea this guy was into cars. And speed. He never mentioned it when I bought my car from him.

"Well, it's…" Dmitri takes a deep breath. He looks at me to see if I'm really interested in knowing, or whether I'm just making conversation. But I'm in. "It's wicked fun," he says. "I go out every Saturday during racing season. We have a pit meeting around noon, and then we do a few sorting runs to figure out which class everybody's going to drag in."

"What do you mean?" I ask. "Don't you already know which class you'll race in?"

Dmitri shakes his head. "Depends on who's racing that day. There's all kinds of cars."

"Like what?"

"Well, there're street cars, like yours. And there are cars like mine, which are stock. There's nothing pro, though."

"What's street?"

"Street? You haven't modded the engine too much. They're pretty much right off the lot. You haven't messed with the carb or the gear ratio or anything like that."

"And so stock means you have?" I ask.

Dmitri nods. "Yeah, like stock could be anything. They're louder, faster. Some have high-efficiency engines. Nitrous and all that."

"Do you do your own…messing?" I ask, pointing to the air intake.

"Modifications?" He nods again. "Some. Like I did the racing stripes and took the rev limiter off, but I had the carburetor done by a guy who knows what he's doing."

My mind buzzes as I add all this new information. I've heard of drag racing, but I've never really thought about doing it, much less met anyone who does.

"So what kind of cars do you race against?" I ask.

"Depends who's there," he says. "There's all kinds. Corvettes, Mustangs like yours, Mazdas. Escalades."

I laugh at that. "Seriously? People race in their Escalades?"

"Sure," he says. "My first race before I modded this engine was against a minivan."

"No!"

"Yeah," he laughs. "It's crazy. I've even seen a station wagon. People just race whatever they've got. It's good times."

I laugh again at the image of mini-vans and station wagons racing each other. I look at him for a moment. I like him. I like the way he talks to me. God, I like the *fact* that he talks to me. No one else does.

But more than that, I like the way it feels to be talking with him.

I look at the car, then back at him.

"Start it up," I say, nodding toward the driver's side. "I want to hear it."

Dmitri looks surprised, but he grins and pulls his keys from his pocket. He unlocks the driver's side and slips inside, leaving the door open. I watch him push in the clutch and turn the key in the ignition. The motor roars into life, splitting the night air. It's so loud! I peek around, suddenly feeling like a troublemaker. An older couple leaving the coffee shop pause to look in our direction.

The noise from the motor thrills me so much that all the little hairs on my arms and the back of my neck are standing up. Dmitri revs the engine a bit. The exhaust responds with a few growling coughs before returning to a throaty idle. My mouth drops open in a ridiculous smile.

I can't contain my excitement. "What's with all the backfiring?" I ask.

Dmitri shrugs from his low seat behind the wheel. "Engine's cold, I guess," he says. He revs it again, just a little bit, and another *boom* erupts from the tailpipe. My grin widens. I wanna ride in that car.

"Take me out," I say.

Dmitri's eyebrows register his surprise. "Definitely," he says. "That'd be cool. May long weekend? We'll make the first day of the season."

I shake my head at him. "No," I say. "Take me now."

Chapter Five

I don't remember the last time I enjoyed myself like this. It feels like years ago.

Even just pulling out of the parking lot onto Desautels Street makes me smile. And now that we're nearing the city limits, the engine loud in our ears and the wind messing our hair, I'm grinning like an idiot.

"How long have you been racing?" I ask. I have to raise my voice to be heard over the engine.

"A while," Dmitri says. "At the track? I guess about a year now."

"What do you like about it?" I ask. "I mean, I know you like going fast, but besides that."

He thinks for a moment. "I like the people," he says. "There are all different kinds. Some of them are really into car stuff, and others are just into speed." He pauses. "I think what I like most is being in tune with my engine. It sounds kind of clichéd, but it's true. I like the feeling of figuring out the exact moment to shift. Trying to find the most power."

Dmitri opens it up a bit as we head off an exit ramp and onto the highway. I love the way his hands look on the wheel. A little thrill flutters loose in my stomach.

Okay, dangerous thoughts. Steering back to cars now.

"So does this car kick ass at the track?" I ask.

Dmitri glances at me and smiles. "It'd kick your car's ass."

"The hell it would!" I say, in mock outrage.

He turns serious. "You're right," he nods. "You'd pound me with your little pony car."

"Damn straight," I say. "I'd wipe the track with your sorry butt."

"That may be." He laughs, and again the sound fills my body, warming me. "Your car's cuter anyway," he says. He looks over again, his hand easy on the gearshift. I'm suddenly aware of how close it is to my leg. I tear my eyes away.

Dmitri goes back to my original question. "Yeah, this car's fast, but speed doesn't really matter. In my class, we all race at pretty much the same pace."

"I don't get it," I say. "Where's the fun in that? Don't you want to blow everyone else away? Isn't that the point?"

"Maybe for street racing. But racing at the track isn't really about beating the other guy," he replies. "It's more about competing with yourself. To get a better time with each run."

"So you're at a racetrack...but you're not there to race against other cars?" I ask. "You just...race against yourself?"

He laughs. "Yeah, that's pretty much it."

I consider this as I look out the window. We've left the city behind. Last year's hay bales sit in the spring-time puddles in the farmers' fields. I try to count the posts on the barbed-wire fences as we pass them by. I used to do that on road trips when I was little. Before my parents split up. But despite being older—and better at counting—the fenceposts still go too fast. I lose track.

I turn back to Dmitri. "Okay then, racer boy," I say. "Give me some tips on how to race at high speeds. Without killing myself."

He smiles at me again, and that little flutter goes off in my tummy. I pretend to be interested in the stereo as he answers. "Stay in control," he says. "And don't take risks any bigger than you can handle."

"That's it? How do you know if you're taking risks that are too big?"

He answers me slowly, enunciating each word deliberately as if I were five years old. "Um, when it starts to feel scary and dangerous?"

I punch his arm. "Listen, you. I'm new at this!" I exclaim.

He laughs. "You're right. I should assume you don't know how to handle yourself in a vehicle. Seeing how you drive a Mustang GT and all."

It's my turn to smile. I like how he thinks I can drive.

We stay out for another hour. We talk about cars and music and work. Mostly Dmitri talks. I'm happy to listen.

"Enough from me," Dmitri finally says, slowing the car. "You want a turn?"

I look around at the road. Ordinarily it would blow my mind to be able to drive a speed machine like this. But tonight? I don't know. I'm kind of cool just chilling here, letting Dmitri have the wheel. Listening.

"Next time," I say.

Next time? a little voice chirps. *When did we decide there'd be a next time, Jenessa?*

Dmitri grins at me. "Next time," he agrees. And then he punches it.

Chapter Six

I guess some part of me decided there'd be a next time after all. Because we do the same thing the next Friday. And the one after that. And the one after that.

The drill: Dmitri and I meet up after work at the coffee shop. I get a serious case of the butterflies. We get a drink and then hit the road. We laugh. We talk about school, cars, jobs. We listen to music.

We talk about ourselves—our habits, our hopes, our histories.

Everything.

There are certain parts that I skip.

"There's this section of the highway down by where I live," I say one evening, shifting my body in the seat so I'm facing him more. "I can see big black streaks on the pavement when I drive by. I think there's street racing going on there."

"Down south, close to 44X?" Dmitri asks. "The road leading to the new developments they're starting to build?"

I nod.

"I'd say you're probably right."

"I bet that'd be fun," I say.

Dmitri looks at me sharply. "You don't want to be doing that," he says. His voice is serious. His eyes are dark. The look in them makes me shiver.

"Why not?" I ask. "Hey, keep your eyes on the road, man."

Dmitri glances at the darkened highway. Then back at me.

"Street racing's dangerous stuff, Jenessa," he says. Another little shiver runs through my body when I hear him say my name.

Of course he'd say that. Who doesn't know that it's dangerous? But only for people who don't know what they're doing.

"Yeah, well, it might be more fun than the track," I counter. "If you're street racing, you don't have to stop after, like, seven seconds or whatever it is." I point to his speedometer. "Your car could probably pound most other cars in the city," I say. "Why don't you try it?"

Dmitri doesn't answer, just presses his lips together. When he finally speaks, he doesn't answer my question.

"It's nothing to mess with," he says.

I give his knee a playful little push. "I'm sure I'd be able to hold my own. I can deal with it. I can drive fast. Just as fast as anyone. And I wouldn't lose control." I smile at him. "And it's fun. *Dangerous*."

Dmitri shakes his head. "I'm sure you could hold your own, given the ideal circumstances. But street racing's far from ideal. And the guys who get involved in it aren't the greatest kinds of people to hang around with."

I fold my arms. "And how do you know all this?"

He pauses. "I watch the news."

"Well, the only time a street-racing gang makes the news is when they get busted," I say.

Dmitri looks at me. "Or hurt."

"But it doesn't happen very often," I say.

"Jenessa." Another shiver. "You can't hook up with a street-racing gang. It isn't safe. They push each other to take stupid risks. Sometimes innocent people get killed."

The shiver gives way to a sickening wave at his words.

Innocent people get killed.

My own words suddenly dry up. I look down at my hands.

"Why do you drive anyway?" he asks. His tone is different now. Less serious.

I shrug.

"You crave the risk?" He glances at me. "The need for speed?" He laughs.

I don't want to talk about this. I reach for his iPod and search around for something different.

I realize I should say something. I don't want him to think I'm choked at something he's said. How could he have known?

I scroll through the playlists, willing my brain toward another topic.

"Hey," I say. "You've got the Spice Girls on here! What's up with *that*?"

Dmitri grabs the iPod from me. "My sister, man! She's ten."

"Well, she's pretty out of touch," I say, grabbing it back. "Tell her to try Justin Bieber or something." Dmitri makes a play for the iPod, but I hold it out of his reach. "Hang on. Let me find something else. How about, um... The Airborne Toxic Event? That sounds kind of exciting. Wait...The Airborne Toxic Ev...is that like a fart?"

He laughs. "Try the Dead Milkmen."

I run my finger down the screen. "'Bitchin' Camaro'?"

"That's the one."

I touch it, and Dmitri cranks the volume. The car fills with crazy punk chords and shouty lyrics.

Without warning, Dmitri floors it. I shriek and then laugh. I can't help myself. Dmitri grins. The Camaro roars forward, chewing up the road, insatiable. I feel my body being pressed back into the seat, hard. I can barely lift my head off the headrest.

I look up at the night sky through the passenger window. Suddenly I get it: a little taste of what I've been looking for.

Freedom.

Chapter Seven

It's not just the night air. It's not just that this is our third week of meeting up after work and going for a drive. It's not just the music that surrounds us, teasing us with its sexy thumping hip-hop vibe. It's not just the excitement of riding in this car, on this seat that sends different vibrations through my body depending on what gear we're in. It's not just that

Dmitri is sitting beside me, his hand on the gearshift and his eyes on the road. It's not just that every time we go out, we talk like we've known each other all our lives. It's not just that tonight Dmitri told me he spends all his time looking forward to Friday night.

It's all of it.

By the time we pull back into the parking lot of the coffee shop at a quarter past one, I'm breathing heavily. My mouth is open and my breath is short. I've never felt so alive. My senses are finely attuned, ready to pick out the slightest noise or sensation. The night air has sharpened my sight and smell.

Dmitri kills the engine and we unbuckle. Usually he lets me off at my car, but tonight he's parked us over on the other side of the lot. Away from the streetlights. Which is fine by me. He turns and looks at me wordlessly. I see in his eyes what I feel in my own body. He reaches for me, and I'm already there. Our lips meet and we're kissing, hot, breathy, tongues slicking across lips, taking in each other's smell, feeling each other's skin. Tasting, for endless minutes. And then harder, more urgent, biting lips and sucking tongues. I've never kissed like this before. Never been kissed like this before. I can't stop myself. I want more. I want this all night. His kiss is intoxicating. I drink it in, greedy for more of this drug that is Dmitri. I can't get enough. Can't get close enough. I want to crawl inside him, to eat him up, to have this feeling forever.

I climb out of my seat and he grabs my hips, pulling me across the console so I'm sitting astride his lap. He buries his hands in my wind-messed hair, kissing my neck, running his tongue along my jaw, biting me. I am completely unhinged, fully at the mercy of this moment. He runs his hands down my back, touching off a nerve center, and I arch toward him, my head back. His lips graze my bra through my T-shirt, and I press against him, wanting everything, right here, right now. I kiss him, soft, inhaling his smell. He pulls away and looks at me, his eyes dark. Unguarded.

I kiss him again. His hands find my stomach, my sides, my back. They're warm, and they're strong, and they're holding me.

I feel safe.

He kisses me again, gently, and suddenly the tears come, hot and silent and unbidden. They sting my eyes, running like thin, scalded streams down the sides of my cheeks. Dmitri kisses them, too, and the more he touches my face, the more I cry. He doesn't ask with his words, just his eyes. And he sees that I'm okay with it, that I don't need to leave or be alone or be not touched. God, no. His touch is the only thing that's keeping me on earth right now, in this storm of emotion-choked insanity. I cry and he kisses me, and then he pulls me close, into his arms, and stays with me, holding me.

I let go—of all the fear and blame and guilt and sadness, of all these long months, of this nightmare I've been living.

"I'm sorry," I whisper. The words come out in heavy hiccuping sobs, and I can't stop them. "I'm sorry. I'm so sorry." And I'm talking to Dmitri, of course I am, but I'm talking to someone else too.

I'm talking to Adrienne.

I let go and lean into Dmitri, and let it run its course, my tongue unable to hold my apologies any longer. He holds my head against his shoulder and strokes my hair. And then he says the words that lift it all from me, even just for a moment.

"I know."

When my tears have dried into sniffles and I'm making sense again, he pulls me away from him to look at me. I'm a mess. My face is hot and puffy, my eyelashes still wet. His eyes are full of understanding.

"You drive," he says, "because you're running." He touches my hair.

And then I tell him.

Chapter Eight

I can't bear to see Dmitri again.

When I wake up the next morning, the cold light of day brings it all home to me. I feel naked, exposed, like I've shared something I never should have.

It's all still there. Nothing's changed. I've still killed my best friend. And telling someone else about it—

even someone as amazing as Dmitri—
doesn't make it better.

In a way, it makes things worse.
Because now all the details that I've
kept locked up so tight over these past
six months are spread all around for
me to examine again. It's like a wound
that's been torn open just when the
stitches were starting to dissolve.

I hate myself for not staying in
control. For letting myself get involved
with someone else.

For letting myself care again.

Dmitri messages me a few times the
following week. But I can't bring myself
to answer him. On Friday, I avoid the
coffee shop after work.

Just after nine thirty, Dmitri texts
me, wondering where I am. A little
while later, another one pings my inbox.

I ignore it. I ignore it, too, when he
calls.

To his credit, he gets it, and stops.

Forget driving with him. I'm better off alone, where I can keep my head about me. Much more balanced.

And forget going to the track with him. I don't need some stupid seven-second sprint to feel my escape. Sure, it might be nice to learn how to make my engine work to its fullest potential, or how to drive with more skill. But I prefer the open road.

Instead of heading to the coffee shop, I make a pit stop at 7-Eleven. Diet Coke and a bag of sunflower seeds.

I drive south, toward where the street racers go. I don't know when these guys usually show up, so I've come prepared to spend some time waiting.

I pull over onto a gravel construction road that connects with the highway. They're still building and developing this neighborhood, which is probably why the street racers come here to do their thing. There's not a lot of traffic, but it's still inside the city limits.

I turn off the engine and climb out, taking my music with me. I grab a blanket from inside the trunk and make my way up the steep berm beside me. At the top, I spread the blanket out, plug in my head-phones and unscrew the cap on the bottle of Coke. From where I sit, I can see the long black tire streaks on the pavement. My stomach tightens a bit when I think I'm about to watch real street racing.

Dmitri would freak if he knew I was here.

I shiver. Then I shake off the thought.

Whatever. Dmitri's not part of the picture anymore. I try to ignore the little fluttering feeling I get in my belly when I think of him.

I settle in to wait.

They show up around one o'clock. Four cars. Three of them are old-school, like Dmitri's, but not as nice. One car's super flashy. It looks like a newer American model, but I can't really tell from here. The guy who's driving it seems to be some sort of leader. He walks with a swagger, and everybody listens to him. They don't move around much when he talks. That's power.

The races get underway. I watch, grinning, as the cars rip down the highway and back, over and over, with a few breaks in between.

It's during one of those breaks that the powerhouse steps away from the group and starts climbing the hill. It takes me a second to realize he's headed my way. I think about my options. Run? It's dark. I'd trip and fall for sure. Stand my ground? But what if he's dangerous? He's totally breaking the law by racing on the streets. Who's to say he's not going to hurt me?

Chapter Nine

Maybe he doesn't even know I'm here. Maybe he's climbing up to get a better view or something.

"What are you doing?" The anger in his voice cuts the night air, and I jump.

Nope. Not looking for a better view.

I fight the urge to look around to see if he's talking to someone else. Of course he isn't. Who else is out here but me?

I take a breath and make sure my voice is steady. I need to seem like I'm in control, not worried. "I'm watching you guys," I say, ignoring my pounding heart. "What else would I be doing up here at two in the morning?"

"Holy shit," he says. I hear a surprised laugh. "You're a chick!"

I don't reply.

"Why aren't you down at the stage, hanging out with us?" he asks. He comes closer, and I can just make his face out. Dark hair. Strong features.

I shrug, although he probably can't see it. I answer his question with one of my own. "How'd you know I was up here?"

He points far along the berm to my left. "We got a guy on lookout. Want to see the cops before they see us."

I look toward where he's pointing, but I can't see a thing. "Oh."

He takes a spot on the blanket next to me. Like he belongs here, in my space.

I'm not sure I like sitting with a complete (lawbreaking) stranger, in the middle of the night, in an unpopulated part of town.

But why else did you come here, Jenessa? You know you wanted to meet them sometime.

You know you want to race.

"You want to come down and watch?" he asks. "You should. We like chicks." He smiles but doesn't look at me. "Don't get many of them around here. And the ones that do come are usually dogs."

There's something that bugs me about the way he says *chick*. And *dog*. I wonder if he ever refers to girls as anything other than animals.

"I kind of like it up here," I say.

He looks at me. "What are you afraid of?" he asks.

I meet his gaze. "Nothing, really," I say.

He smiles again, at me this time. He sticks out his hand. "Cody."

I look at his hand, then at him. His smile is a bit tight. Different than Dmitri's. Which is all I've been able to think about this past week, damn him. All I want to do is forget about him.

Maybe this guy can help me out.

I take Cody's hand. "Jenessa."

"You want to race, Jenessa?"

I shrug. "Not really," I lie. "Just like watching."

He studies me for a minute. "Bullshit," he says. "You want to race."

I can't help but laugh. It's exactly the thing I would say. I look at him. He's sizing me up, a gleam of a challenge in his eyes.

"Maybe I do," I say. "But maybe I'll just watch."

Cody jumps to his feet and holds out his hand to pull me up. "Then at least come and watch where there's beer and lawn chairs. It's cold in the wind up here." He looks around. "And you don't have anything to drink, that I can see."

I point to my half-finished bottle of Diet Coke.

He shrugs. "If you call that a drink."

I consider his offer. "All right," I say. I stand, ignoring his outstretched hand, and draw my jacket around me. He leaves his hand there for a second to make the point that I've been rude in not accepting it.

I pick up my blanket and Diet Coke.

Cody shrugs and shoves his hands into his pockets. He leads the way down the hill. "Where's your car?" he asks.

I motion toward the bottom of the hill. "Parked around on the construction road."

He nods. "Whatcha got?"

"Sorry?"

"Your car, duh," he says. "What do you drive?"

"A GT 2003," I say, rankled at his comment. Guess he was getting me back for rejecting him up on the hilltop.

I can't resist. "What do you drive, *duh*?"

He stops so suddenly that I almost bump into him. He turns around to face me. I feel a tiny spiral of fear start to twist in my belly. He looks at me for a moment. Then he smiles, but it doesn't touch his eyes. "You're a tough chick, Jenessa. I like that."

He points toward where all the cars are lined up in the ditch, just out of sight. A few guys are leaning against an old convertible, talking and laughing. "Mine's the Viper, 2009."

"Nice," I say. I mean it. It's a beautiful car.

"You got that right," he says.

We join the group, and Cody introduces me around. Mike, Mark, Rishad, some guy whose nickname is Bibs. They say hi and give me quick smiles.

Cody bends to take a bottle of beer from a cooler on the ground.

He turns to me and winks. "A mustang and a viper, huh? That's quite the hot little combo. I think they go pretty well together." He takes my hand. I let him have it, but not before he feels my instinctive reflex to pull away. He pulls me closer, forcing me to take a step toward him. I fight the urge to pull back. Instead I go bold, letting him get close.

Cody looks at me. His eyes are a clear green, beautiful, like the ocean, but they're cool. I look right into them, not flinching. He pulls me a fraction of a step closer. "You *are* a wild little mustang," he says. I stiffen, my danger radar flicking quickly from yellow to orange.

Then he holds my arm out. "Relax, Jenessa," he says. "I'm just offering you a beer." He places the cold bottle in my hand.

I close my fingers around it, gripping it to stop my hand from shaking. "Thanks," I say.

The conversation near the other car has died away. The other guys are kind of watching without trying to seem like they're watching.

Part of me is telling myself to get in my car and *leave*, to not come back here again.

And another, bigger part is thrilled to be here, this close to danger. With a guy who definitely feels like someone I shouldn't be hanging out with. Who feels a bit dangerous himself.

And who's not Dmitri.

"Want some help with that?" Cody asks, nodding toward the cap on my bottle of beer. It's tight.

I narrow my eyes at him and laugh. "As if," I say. But I keep my tone light.

I snatch a corner of my jacket and reef on the cap, hoping it'll give and that I won't look like an idiot.

The cap pops off. I drop it on the pavement and knock back half the bottle in three seconds. Bless my father for showing me how to open my throat and guzzle Kool-Aid when I was eleven years old. I'm sure he has no idea how useful I've found it.

"Wow, *yeah!*" says the Bibs guy. He claps, and a couple others laugh.

I take the bottle from my lips. Cody watches. I level my gaze at him. "So? You gonna race, big guy?" I smile sweetly. "Or are you going to stand around staring at me all night?"

Laughter erupts from the group gathered around the convertible, but it ebbs quickly. Cody doesn't turn to look. He doesn't say anything either. He's not happy with me stealing his thunder.

At the same time, I can see that he likes the challenge I'm laying down. I bet there aren't a lot of people who give Cody a hard time. And chances are, if I knew him better, I might not do it either.

But for now, ignorance is bliss.

I stay until the last race of the night. At the end of the evening, as everyone's packing up, Cody comes close. He smells like beer and engine oil.

"I'll see you next week," he says.

It's not an invitation so much as an order. But I nod. I want to come back. I want to watch the racing. And, strangely, I want more of Cody.

As I drive home, I touch the sore spots on my neck where he grabbed me for a kiss.

I wonder if he left a mark.

Chapter Ten

I'm waiting when Mark and Bibs pull in. Cody follows a few minutes later. I've parked just off the shoulder, like everyone else.

I lean against Cody's car, and we watch a few races. Mark and Mike. Bibs and some new guy, Doran. The guys are always careful to make sure the road is clear before they take off. From the starting line, you can see almost a mile in each direction. When there are no lights coming, they go. And they rotate the lookout every couple of hours. No one wants the cops hassling us.

Cody hands me a new beer every time I finish one. With him, it seems drinking isn't really an option. It's more like an expectation. I think he's on his fifth.

He's standing beside me now, his arm draped carelessly around my waist. I kind of like it. The beer has loosened me up, worn down my sharp edges. I find myself shrieking and laughing every time the cars peel off the line in a scream of rubber.

After my third beer, my vision has grown fuzzy. I reach for my cigarettes and light up. I hadn't planned on letting Cody in on my dirty little secret, but I'm feeling good tonight. And I feel like having a smoke.

I take a drag, careful to blow the smoke away from Cody. I hope he doesn't say anything.

Maybe I'll offer him one.

I take another puff and turn to see his hand moving toward my face, fast. I flinch backward. My other hand comes up to shield my face.

Cody laughs. The sound is hard. He takes the cigarette from my mouth with a sharp little yank. "Relax, Jenessa," he says. "You're so tense. Did you think I was going to hit you or something?"

Funny, that's exactly what I thought. My heart is racing.

"You shouldn't smoke. It's bad for your health." He holds the burning cigarette just out of reach.

Now it's my turn to laugh. His words are absurd. "Oh, and drinking and driving isn't?" I say. It spills out before I can stop it. But I'm pissed that he scared me like that.

Cody looks at me for a moment, then throws the cigarette onto the pavement. He ignores my question. "Put it out," he says. His face is dark. "That shit's toxic. I don't want it stinking up my stage."

I can't believe this. Stinking up his stage? Who does this guy think he is?

I don't like being pushed around. "I'll go finish this somewhere else," I say, bending down to pick up the smoke. "Where it won't bother you."

He lowers his boot onto my hand. Gently.

"I said, *put it out*."

The other guys are watching, shifting nervously. My face reddens with shame. But I don't want to make him angrier.

"Okay." It comes out sounding weak. "*Okay*," I say, louder. "Get off me."

He takes his foot off my hand. I stand up without looking at him. I step on the burning end and grind it out with my shoe. I want to say something nasty, something to put him in his place and tell him that I don't like the way he's treating me. But I can't predict his reactions. He's freaky. I don't know what he'll let go of—and what'll flip him out.

As soon as I've put the cigarette out, Cody's all friendly again. I lean against the car beside him, and he puts his arm back around me.

I'm sickened when I realize I feel relieved.

A few minutes pass without us talking, and then he offers me another beer. I say no.

"What do you mean, *no*?" he asks.

I'm careful to choose the right words. I don't want to make it seem like I'm accusing him of anything. "I mean," I say slowly, "if I drink any more, I won't be able to drive."

"Sure you will," he says, moving to stand in front of me. "You'll just go faster." His tone is playful. He grins and slides his hands down to my butt.

Wow.

He's not at all the same guy I saw a few minutes ago. He presses himself against me and nuzzles my neck.

I can't help it. I smile.

Then he kisses me. It's not like Dmitri's kiss, not by a long shot, but I find my body responding to him of its own accord. I like feeling his hands around my hips, his rough stubble on my chin. No butterflies with this guy. Instead, my stomach sends out a warning signal.

Danger.

I ignore it. Give me the danger. I'll take it. *I'm no lightweight.*

Unbidden, the words pop into my brain.

I bite my lip against sudden tears.

I grab Cody's butt and press into him. I pull him closer. He kisses me hard, liking my body language.

But when he moves to put his hands under my shirt, something in my core shifts. I feel sick, nauseated.

I put my hands over his to stop them. I think as fast as my beer-fuzzed brain will let me. I don't want to offend or embarrass him, so I think about my words.

"Not here," I say, nodding toward the others. I fake a smile and punch him lightly on the chest to soften my message.

I catch something in his eyes, and the signals in my gut go all weird. I don't understand what I want. My heart is beating fast.

I want him to kiss me again. I want to be stupid.

Danger.

I lean forward again, but he just laughs.

"Let's go."

"Go?" I parrot.

"Yeah, let's race."

I blink. "What? Right now? I can't drive like this." If I'm not over the limit, then I'm definitely close to it. And I'm not even legal yet.

Cody stares at me for a moment, then shrugs. "Suit yourself." He drops his hands and steps away from me. I watch as he takes a pull on the beer that's in his hand. I can feel the chill coming off him.

I suddenly feel empty.

I stick around for a while and try to talk with him. But his answers get shorter and shorter. I go to talk with the other guys, but it's obvious they don't want to have much to do with me if Cody's mad.

I'm angry that I'm making a mess of everything. Including my own brain.

I watch one more race, standing alone by Cody's car.

Almost everybody has been eliminated from tonight's showdown.

Cody and Bibs will be the last race of the night.

Cody doesn't even acknowledge me as he climbs into his seat and starts the engine.

Stumbling a bit from the beer, I leave.

Chapter Eleven

I shouldn't go back down there. I feel
stupid and small and embarrassed after
last week's disagreement with Cody.
But I still want to race.

And—damn it—I want to see Cody.
I feel like I disappointed him last week.

I take a few beers from the fridge
and leave the house around midnight.
Dad's out at some meeting. I'm nervous

about how Cody will treat me when I show up, so I pop the top on one of the bottles. It'll take the edge off. That, and a bit of music. And maybe a smoke.

The early summer air feels warm on my face as I drive down to the stage. I park on the shoulder and wait. I take a wet wipe out of the packet I bought earlier in the week and scrub my fingers so Cody can't smell the cigarette.

My mixed messages start up again. Maybe he won't show up tonight. Maybe that would be a good thing. The guy's got to take a day off every now and then, right?

Right.

I feel a mixture of fear and excitement when he pulls up. First car of the night.

He kills the engine and climbs out. Motions for me to do the same. And, like a robot, I do. He doesn't even say hello, just grabs the back of my neck

and presses his mouth against mine.
My air leaves me in a sharp gasp and
he leans into me against the side of my
car, pressing his pelvis into me. I tip
my head back, and he pushes his hands
into my hair.

"You're so beautiful," he whispers
against my throat. "I missed you." A
shiver works its way from the bottom of
my spine all the way out to my fingertips. His hands find their way under my
shirt. I don't try to stop him this time.

I'm no lightweight.

I lean into Cody, wanting to please
him. He unbuttons my jeans and slips
his hand inside, rough. But I can live
with it. He likes it.

And that makes me happy.

I hardly notice when another car
pulls up. But Cody does. He pulls back
suddenly, leaving me to yank my shirt
down over my unbuttoned pants in the
glare of the other car's headlights.

I turn my back. My hands shake as I quickly zip my jeans and button them. My face burns. Shame prickles in my throat.

Isn't this what you wanted, Jenessa?

My head's spinning, and I've only had one beer.

Cody goes around to the passenger side of his car and pulls out his cooler of beer. He throws one in my direction. I forget about trying to straighten my shirt and grab for the bottle. I don't want it to hit the ground. Who knows how mad he'd be if I let that happen.

He laughs.

The night has begun.

Chapter Twelve

"Hey, Jenessa. How's by you?"

My hcart stops whcn I hcar Dmitri's voice. I didn't check the caller ID before picking up. I was assuming it'd be a telemarketer.

I figured Dmitri had given up on me. It's been weeks since that night we parked. Weeks since I turned into a blubbering idiot in front of him.

"I'm...good," I say. "Busy." I pause. "Midterms and all."

Dmitri laughs. The sound of it loosens something inside me. Releases a tightness in my chest that I didn't even know was there.

"Yeah," he says. "Exams suck. Studying hard?"

I pause. I bite my tongue against a sudden desire to tell him how sorry I am for blowing him off.

"Yeah," I say. "I'm almost through them now though."

"Well, that's good," he says. "Maybe we can get out to the track yet." I can hear the smile in his voice. Why does he have to be so goddamned friendly?

I glance at the clock. I'm due out at the stage in half an hour. Cody's expecting me. I don't want to be late.

The tightness returns.

I close my eyes and rub them with one hand. "Maybe," I answer.

I know I'm blowing Dmitri off again. It's so rude. I'm angry with myself. With him for calling me. For making me be mean to him.

I want to throw something.

I force myself to take a deep breath. "Dmitri," I say.

He doesn't wait for me. "I haven't seen you around much," he says. His voice is quieter, serious. "Actually, I haven't seen you around at all."

The doorbell rings. Probably the wilderness people raising funds again for that pipeline ban. I grab a twenty-dollar bill off the counter.

Oil baron to the rescue, I think, and almost smile.

I swipe my hair back behind my shoulder and walk toward the front entrance.

"You still drinking Americanos?" Dmitri's asking me.

Weird question. "Uhmm…," I say, opening the door.

And there he is. Standing right in front of me, on my doorstep. Smiling, his phone up to his ear.

The phone slips right out of my hand. It bounces off my leg and lands on the rug.

Dmitri closes his phone and slides it into his pocket. Looks at the money in my hand.

"Oh. You don't have to pay me for it," he says. He winks and holds out one of the two cups he's holding. "It's on me. Extra hot, just like you take it."

I smile. But then I remember that I'm not supposed to want to see him. My smile morphs into a weird sort of grimace.

I reach for the cup to save him from looking dumb. His fingers brush mine, and I end up snatching the cup from his hand.

My next words make me seem like even more of a bitch.

"Listen," I say. "I gotta run. I'm sorry. I have to be somewhere in a few minutes."

God, you haven't even said hello. Or thanked him for the coffee. Could you maybe be just a *little* bit ruder?

A shadow of disappointment crosses Dmitri's face, but his recovery is gracious. "Need a lift?"

I glance over his shoulder at the Camaro parked at the end of my driveway. My tummy does a little loopy thing when I see it. I think about driving with Dmitri. Kissing him.

Bawling my eyes out in front of him.

Telling him everything.

I look back at him. "No. I'll be needing my own car tonight." My tone is sharper than I mean it to be, but maybe it's just as well. I just want him to go away and forget about me.

So that I can forget about him.

Dmitri's face doesn't register any emotion. "You're racing," he says. It's not a question.

"Maybe I am."

He looks away for a second, then back at me. "That's dangerous stuff, Jenessa. I told you, people get killed doing that."

As soon as the words leave his mouth, he realizes his mistake.

I swallow.

"I'm sorry," he says. He looks down. "I'm sorry. I just…I don't want to see you hurt."

"You don't have to worry about me."

"Pretty hard not to with the idiots who're running that show," he says. "I know those guys."

My eyes narrow. He never told me that before.

And it bothers me that he's dissing Cody and his friends.

It also bothers me that he's right.

My mixed-up feelings make me even angrier. "I happen to like them," I say. "What, did they kick you out or something?"

He shakes his head.

"Said you were too wholesome, maybe?" I snap.

Dmitri stares at me.

"Oh, *I* know," I say, tilting my head to the side and looking at him. "You were too chicken to run with them, weren't you, Dmitri?" Boy, I'm on a roll now. Jackknife Jenessa, right in your face. "Little too safety-oriented, should we say?"

This finally punctures his cool veneer. Anger flickers in his eyes. He opens his mouth to speak. His eyes meet mine and hold me there for a few seconds. Then he looks down at the cup in his hands. He releases a long breath.

When he looks back at me, his eyes are almost calm.

"Right," he says. "Well, have a good night then."

I watch, my throat aching, as he walks down the driveway and gets into his car.

Don't go, Dmitri. Come back.

The words are in my head, but I can't get them into my mouth.

I'm sorry.

He starts the Camaro up. Steers it out of the cul-de-sac without looking back. I wait for the sound of his engine to disappear before closing the door.

I jam my feet into my flip-flops and grab a hoodie. Snatch my keys off the hook.

I stare at my reflection in the full-length mirror for a long time. Then I give it the finger.

And then I throw my extra-hot Americano at it.

I slam the door behind me, leaving the coffee to drip like dark tears.

Chapter Thirteen

A couple of weeks later, I've raced a few times. Tires squealing, engines throbbing, hands sweating on the wheel. I take on the whole gang, one by one, and even though they dust me every time, I have fun. The guys are generous with their encouragement.

Most of them.

I'm standing with Cody on a warm night in May, pleasantly buzzed off a few beers. I'm trying not to think about the fact that Dmitri had suggested I go to the track with him this weekend to kick off the drag season.

We're late getting started tonight. Everyone's enjoying themselves, talking and drinking. Cody's running his hand up and down my back under my shirt. He's in a good mood tonight.

He tosses his empty into the cooler and looks at me, his eyes glittering. "You're up," he grins. "First race tonight."

I laugh and shake my head. "No way," I say, pointing to my stomach. "Too many beers in this belly. I gotta wait awhile."

He ignores my words. Instead, he leans over and puts his mouth to my ear. His breath tickles when he whispers,

"Let's show these pussies what you're *really* made of. Just me and you. Pull it out and show them how kick-ass you are."

I feel a glow that he thinks I'm good. But I don't want to race right now. I'm drunk.

I smile and turn to kiss him. "Don't want a DUI, thanks," I tease.

He pulls back and looks around. "I don't see any pigs here. Do you?"

I glance around us. A few cars have passed, but that was a while ago. No one's on the road now. The lookout would have signaled, anyway, if he'd seen cops.

"Nope. No pigs." But I still don't want to get behind the wheel.

And I have a feeling he isn't going to make it easy for me.

I scramble for a way to handle this before it gets heavy. "You go, babe. I want to watch you race Rishad now that he's turbocharged his engine." I lay on a bit of flattery to sweeten my rejection. "You'll still punk his ass."

Cody stiffens, and I know the conversation's headed the wrong way. He raises his voice. "I said, I don't see any cops," he says. He addresses the group standing over Rishad's car. "Any of you guys see any police out here tonight? Huh?" He squeals loudly, startling me. "See any pigs?"

"No pigs, boss," says Mark quickly. "We're clear."

Cody looks back at me. His mouth is turned up at one corner. His voice is soft. My stomach twists. I don't like it when he talks this way. Usually it means something is about to happen. Last week he talked like this just before he pushed me. It wouldn't have been a big deal, except I was standing on the edge of the shoulder, where the ditch dropped off behind me. So when he shoved me, I lost my balance and fell backward and hit my head. It wasn't so bad. I only got a couple of scratches from the rocks. And my goose egg was mostly gone by the next morning. It took me a second to get up after he'd pushed me though, and I could see that made him angrier. It took a bit of work to chill him out again.

He's been in a good space for most of the night tonight. I don't want to mess it up by arguing.

So I nod. "No police?" I fake a smile. "Then you're on, big guy."

Danger.

As I get behind the wheel, I send up a silent prayer. I kick off my flip-flops and throw them into the backseat. Cody pulls up to the line beside me. Revs his engine. He grins at me, and I force another smile. Bibs gives the signal, and we take off, squealing and roaring. As soon as the car's in motion, I relax. This isn't so bad, after all. Alcohol or no,

I know what I'm doing. I'll never win against Cody, but that's no reason I can't give him a run for his money.

When I hit third gear, I look over to find him grinning. I stick my tongue out at him and punch it, jumping forward and putting a car length between us. Then more.

I glance in the rearview mirror to check Cody's position. My heart drops.

Flashing red and blue. Where did they come from? What the hell was the lookout doing?

I watch in horror as the police cruiser roars up and out of the ditch in a spray of rocks, dirt…and branches. Camouflage. They were waiting for this.

Instinctively, I downshift and jam the pedal to the floor.

I'm no lightweight.

I laugh crazily. I glance in the mirror again, terrorized and yet super-charged. Sharpened.

But I feel sick at what I see next. Cody's dropped back. Way back. I watch, unbelieving, as he kills his lights and turns around so he's heading the other way. Back in the direction we came from. My breath sticks in my throat.

The prick's leaving me out here to deal with this on my own.

I hammer. I've never driven so fast in my life. But I've never been chased. either. If I was thinking straight, I'd have stopped as soon as I saw the cop car and taken the rap. But I'm not thinking straight. And it's too late to stop now.

I don't know where I'm going. I just need to get away.

My pulse races as I fly down the empty highway. The cop's turned on his siren now. I can hear it over the wind and the engine. It fills my ears and pumps my body full of adrenaline. My hands are slick on the wheel. I want to look and see how fast I'm going, but I don't dare take my eyes off the road. If I get caught, I'm done. Not only am I speeding, but I've been drinking. And I'm only sixteen.

My father will kill me. He'll take my car away.

Then I'll die for sure.

Exit signs whip past. I make a split-second decision, tearing off the main highway and onto a ramp. I let off the gas and downshift before I hit the curve, forcing the engine to slow the wheels. My tires shriek as we squall around the corner. I fishtail coming out of the turn. I let off the gas for a second to get the tires back under me.

There's another exit up ahead, and I gun for it. The cops are still behind me, but the ramp slowed them down. I charge toward the next set of ramps and peel myself off onto a smaller road. Yellow dotted lines flash past.

Juice it, baby. Go.

The car responds, growling as I punch through the gears, trying to put as much distance as I can between me and the squad car.

I don't know how long I drive like this. The road narrows. No more yellow lines. Just black asphalt.

My rearview tells me the cops have let it go. They don't want some stupid kid killing herself just because they gave chase. They usually back off if they can't catch their target. That way, they don't cause any accidents.

Innocent people get killed.

Something inside me cracks when I hear Dmitri's words. My eyes blur, and I take a big breath.

Get ahold of yourself, Jenessa. Slow it down.

Gradually, I ease off the gas. But it's too late.

I've already hit the gravel.

Chapter Fourteen

My headlights don't pick up where the pavement ends and where the gravel starts.

I feel my back end start to slide, and I jump off the gas. My rear whips from side to side, spraying thick gravel from under the tires. Dark bushes blur past. I don't remember how to correct a gravel slide.

Terrified, I tap my brakes.

Wrong.

Suddenly I'm spinning out, turning in circles, watching everything in slow motion. The steering wheel slips through my hands like it's got a mind of its own. My headlights splash across a fencepost, then a bush. The road. Another fencepost. Another bush. The road.

I spin for what feels like an eternity before I come to a crunching stop. The force of the impact jerks me sideways. A mass of white nylon explodes in my face, absurdly surprising. My seatbelt sears as it bites into my shoulder. Then I'm slammed back, against my seat.

I wait for my life to flash before my eyes. Isn't that what they say happens? That you see scenes of your life playing out as you die?

Wait. Maybe I should look for the bright white light instead.

I hear a metallic *ping* as a rock bounces off the car.

Then it's quiet.

I open my eyes—I didn't even know they were closed—and look down. Am I still here? My body is here. No blood. Can I feel my hands? Yes. My feet? Yes. I scrabble at the air bag, suddenly frantic to get its parachute-like bulk off me.

My head aches. I raise a shaky hand to touch it. No blood there either.

The cops! Panicked, I look in the rearview mirror. But then I remember. They gave up the chase a long way back.

My back window is blackened, covered with something.

It's blood.

I scream.

How could it be blood? Holy, Jenessa. Bring it down a notch.

I shake my head to clear it. I turn around in my seat and find that the car is jammed, butt-first, into one of the thick hedges lining the road. Leaves cover the rear windows. My engine's off, but my headlights point across the road, lighting up the posts of a barbed-wire fence on the other side.

Saved by a shrub.

I close my eyes again and rest my head. I stay that way for a long time.

I need a smoke.

I open my eyes and look around. One of my flip-flops is on the dash. My cigarettes are on the passenger-side floor, jumbled up with all the other stuff that sprayed out of my purse when I crashed. I grab them and paw through the pile for my lighter. It takes me three tries with hands that are shaking, but I manage to pick up the lighter too. The red light on my BlackBerry is flashing.

Leave a message, I think. I'm busy.

Then I laugh. I laugh and laugh like a broken windup toy, high and shrill and never-ending.

Eventually I stop. The silence folds in again, pressing on me.

I'm suddenly seized by panic. The sense that I'm drowning. I need air.

I need to get *out* of here!

I open my door, half afraid I won't be able to climb out. But I do. Literally. Climb out. My legs won't hold me up. They're working, but they refuse to straighten, refuse to stand. It doesn't occur to me to watch out for other cars as I crawl around on the road. I crab-clutch around in a half circle until my back is leaning up against the driver's-side door.

With fingers that feel as thick as tree trunks, I fumble at the flip-top on the pack of cigarettes. My fingers won't work. They disobey my commands. In frustration, I smash one fist across the top of the pack, and the cigarettes fly out, scattering on the gravel in front of me. I have to use two hands to pick one up. It breaks. I bulldoze back in for another one. It gets bent, but I manage to put it between my lips, where it shakes. *Jibber jibber jibber.*

I grab my lighter—trusty Zippo, lights in rain or wind—and spin the flint wheel with my wooden fingers. Miraculously, it lights. The end of my cigarette dances around, dipping in and out of the golden flame in my hands. I try holding it, but I can't still myself enough to light it.

Enraged, I yank the cigarette out and chuck it away. I throw the lighter, too, as far as I can. It lands with a solid thump somewhere in the tall grass.

Like I'll find that again.

I struggle to my feet, furious at myself. I try to take a step, but my legs feel like they're made of lead. I kick at the cigarettes that litter the road, breaking them and scattering them farther.

Screw it, I think at them. I'm done with you then.

I kick at the gravel. Then I bend down and grab up a scoop of it. I throw it. I do it again. And again. Dimly, I realize that I'm screaming.

When I've cleared away all the gravel I can reach, I stop. My arms are tired. My throat is sore. My face is hot. I lean my back against the car, breathing heavily.

The silence returns, pressing against my head, my ears, my brain. I see Adrienne.

Adrienne, who always went along with me when I pushed her to take stupid risks.

Adrienne, who never said no to my challenges.

Adrienne, who wanted to prove to me that she was up to it. Who didn't want to disappoint me or make me angry.

Adrienne, who could be here right now. But isn't. Because of me.

My legs buckle under me. I slide down the side of the car until I'm sitting on the ground again.

There, with the first pink of dawn warming the horizon, I bury my face in my hands and cry.

Chapter Fifteen

That's it. I'm out.

I'm going to come back out to the stage next week and tell Cody I'm done. He's a jerk anyway. Too bad I didn't recognize it sooner. Well, I did, but…

What the hell was that, turning tail as soon as the cops showed up?

I shudder to think of the excuses I've made for his behavior. The pushing.

The name-calling. The rough touching and kissing that left me violated instead of turned on. Giving me no choice but to drink, and then forcing me to drive.

Ness, he never forced you. You did all that because you didn't want to make him angry. These are the choices you've made.

Yeah, well. I'm making new choices now. And I choose to tell Cody to go take a flying leap.

I wipe my face on my shirt and look around. I'm amazed that no one seems to use this road. Then again, it's six in the morning. Who's going to be out at this time on a Saturday?

I heave myself to my feet and look at the car. I apologize to it, stroking its already cooling metal as I take a walk around. There's not much damage, actually. Other than a couple of big scratches against the rear fender and across the trunk, it looks okay. No flat tires.

I climb into the driver's side and start it up. The engine catches right away. I breathe a sigh of relief.

I ease out of the hedge with a crunching, scraping sound and turn toward home. Ahead of me, the sky is orange. The sun's pink rays are hitting the high clouds, lighting them up like fish scales. It's bloody beautiful.

I am thankful, so thankful, to be alive.

Why do *I* get another chance?

I catch it just in time, slamming on the brakes and flinging open my door.

Right there, in the middle of the road, with the new day in front of me and the old one behind, I puke until my chest hurts.

I'm going to tell Cody I'm out. And then I'll call Dmitri to apologize. There's no reason he should forgive me for being so unkind, but I want to try.

I want to do things the right way from now on.

On the following Friday, I pull into the stage. I'm shivering a bit. Worried about how Cody will take the news.

Then I remember. I have no reason to be nervous. If anyone does, it's him. He's the one who bailed on *me* last week when the cops turned up. He must know I'm pissed.

I get out of the car and wait for Cody. He's talking with Mark. Not so much as a glance my way. He takes his sweet time to finish his conversation, and then he turns and saunters toward me with a half grin.

Headlights splash us as another car arrives.

Cody looks, and his grin falters. I glance behind me at the car that's pulling in.

My breathing stops when I see what it is.

A '69 Camaro.

Chapter Sixteen

"Dmitri!" I say as he climbs out.

Cody looks from Dmitri to me. "You know this guy?" he asks me.

I ignore him. "What are you doing here?"

"Seeing if you're okay," Dmitri replies. "Which I'm not sure you are."

I'm thunderstruck. "How did…" I shake my head. "How did you know I was here?"

He raises his eyebrows.

Oh. Right.

Cody's voice is sharp. "How do you know this guy?" He's talking to me, but his eyes are on Dmitri.

Dmitri answers him. "I'd say we know each other pretty intimately," he says. "Wouldn't you, Jenessa?" His eyes are locked on Cody. I feel a rush of warmth at his words.

But they're the wrong ones for Cody's ears.

When Cody speaks, his voice is different than usual. Tighter.

"Get off my turf, Dmitri," he says.

Dmitri shakes his head. Smiles a little.

Man, he's brave.

"Still mine, Cody. Remember?" he says. "You never earned it."

Silence has fallen around the beer cooler. The other guys are watching the two alpha males circle each other, teeth bared.

"You *gave it up*," Cody snarls.

"I prefer to think I outgrew it," Dmitri replies. "I see you haven't been so lucky."

Cody grabs me, holding me tight with his arm around my waist. I try to step away from him, but he's got me locked.

He's telling me I'm going to pay for this later.

Dmitri looks at me. I try to send him a message with my eyes, but I know there's no way he would understand it. Not with the way I treated him last week.

Dmitri looks back at Cody, but not before I see the hurt.

Then I speak. "It's nothing, Dmitri." I shake my head slowly, my eyes on his.

"This"—I look at Cody —"is *nothing*." My voice cracks on the word.

I feel Cody stiffen and look at me.

"What the hell are you saying?" he says. "What do you mean, this is *nothing*?" I feel his hand draw itself into a fist. "I *made* you, bitch. You owe me." He spins me to face him.

Suddenly I snap. I jerk my hips away from Cody's iron grasp. Shove my face into his. "I don't owe you *any*thing," I hiss. "I made myself. *Bitch*."

The shock on Cody's face is almost comical. He stands with his fists balled up by his sides. Fighting himself.

Dmitri looks at me for a long moment, then nods. Once.

Maybe I was wrong. Maybe he does understand something about this.

Something about me.

He nods toward Cody's car. "Got a nice set there," he says.

Cody's head whips in Dmitri's direction. "Better than your disco piece of shit," he growls.

Dmitri smiles. "Think so? What've you got? A few hamsters in there?"

I hear Bibs bark a laugh behind me. He grunts when someone elbows him in the ribs.

"Dmitri…," I say. He doesn't hear me.

Cody's eyes narrow at Dmitri's comment. I can see him shaking. This isn't good. I've never felt him so angry. I can smell his sweat. Sharp and acrid.

Cody takes a step toward Dmitri. His shoulder hits me, hard. I stumble back but catch myself on my car.

He walks toward Dmitri until they're no more than half a foot apart. In a low voice, he speaks two words that fill me with terror.

"Get in."

No! *No!*

My brain screams the word over and over, but my tongue refuses to unglue itself from the roof of my mouth. Like I'm in a dream, I watch Dmitri walk back to his car and slide in behind the wheel.

No! Dmitri, I'm done! I'm out! I'm not racing anymore. I only came to tell Cody that I'm finished!

This is for me. He's doing this for me.

Because I said he was afraid.

Because he wants to show me he's up to it. That he'll take the risk to prove it to me.

What kind of monster am I?

I feel sick.

But no. I know better. I know now that he *is* a street racer, that he ruled the scene. *This* scene. And that he left this scene…and moved on.

He doesn't have to prove *anything* to me. He already has. So much.

The Camaro roars to life. It punches through my foggy thinking. "Dmitri!" I scream.

I have to tell him how wrong I've been.

I start toward his car. Suddenly the world is spinning around me. I have to bend down and put my head between my knees so I don't pass out. I will myself not to puke. I hear Mark's voice. I feel his hands, helping to steady me.

When I look up again, Rishad's stepping up with the flag. I burst into tears and throw Mark off. I run toward the cars, desperate to talk some sense into Dmitri.

I can't let him go out there alone.

Chapter Seventeen

Rishad drops the flag. The two cars burn out, squalling, leaving me on the line, panting and sobbing.

"Hey." Rishad appears beside me. "Ness. It's cool. Let them go." He puts his arm around me. "This has been a long time coming."

"No!" I scream. I throw off his arm and he backs away, palms raised.

"Okay, okay," he says. His voice is soothing.

"No!" I shriek again. "This. Is. Not. Happening!" I stomp my foot with each word. "This is not *happening*!" I snatch the flag from Rishad's hand and throw it onto the road. It clatters away into the darkness.

I sound like a lunatic, even to my own ears.

I whirl and run for my car. Mark's voice follows me, shouting at me to stop. I yank open the door and slam myself into the seat, starting it up. I roar away from the shoulder, narrowly missing Rishad as I dive onto the highway.

The road lines flash past as I tear along. I don't have a hope of catching them. I don't know what I'd do even if I could. But I can't just…wait. And do nothing.

The taillights rocketing along ahead of me draw farther away, but I can still see both cars clearly. Just when I'm thinking they've reached the end line, I see Cody take a sharp swipe at Dmitri's car.

Is he…? But that car is Cody's baby!

Their side panels connect. I watch, horrified, as the Camaro jerks sideways. Toward the concrete median.

"*No!*" I scream.

Cody backs off, then rams Dmitri again. I'm crying now, the tears slick on my face. Salty on my lips. Cody holds Dmitri, grinding against him. I'm close enough to hear the crunching sound their side panels make as they connect. Metal on metal. I scream again as Cody pushes the Camaro toward the center divide.

I watch in horror as Dmitri swerves inward, closer toward the concrete blocks. What the hell is he doing? He's going to kill hims—

SMASH! Dmitri whips away from the median. Cody takes a hit. His car skips, but he doesn't hit the brakes.

This is going to get ugly.

I see Cody veer out, toward the edge of the highway. I know what he's thinking. He's going to wind up and plow Dmitri. And Dmitri's going to crash into the median.

And then he's going to die.

He's doing this for me.

Cody comes back for the kill.

"*N-o-o-o-o-o-o*!" The word roils up, torn from the center of my core, bursting from my throat in a hysteria-fueled wail that goes on and on without stopping.

I see the skier again, plowing into Adrienne.

I'm no lightweight.

I see her skidding across the snow, pushed by the force of his strike.

Lesser boarders get hurt.

I see the tree in front of her, her body hurtling toward its unyielding solidness.

Innocent people get killed.

I see—

No!

Dmitri's brake lights.

What?

I let off the gas. Dmitri falls back. I slow, keeping pace behind him. My heart is thrumming out some sort of crazy tribal rhythm, but I feel my airway open up a bit. He's falling back.

Bowing out.

Expecting to find Dmitri but finding nothing but open air, Cody's car lunges toward the median. He corrects, but not before his front end grazes the concrete dividers. A shower of sparks erupts from his nose.

And then I see a beautiful thing.

A police cruiser—probably the same one that chased me last week—bursts from the ditch behind us. He rips past us without a sidelong glance, pounding after Cody's car with his lights on and siren blaring.

I feel a stab of relief. They're not after me. Or Dmitri.

The relief gives way to a sudden delicious satisfaction.

If they catch that asshole, they're going to crush his ride.

If he doesn't crush himself first, I think, and shudder.

In front of me, Dmitri slows some more. I follow suit.

He pulls off on the shoulder and I roll to a stop behind him, shaking. My entire body is shaking like I've been shot full of nerve poison. The tremors roll out of my center, one after another, causing my teeth to chatter and my hands to tremble on the wheel.

I fumble with my parking brake and take my foot off the clutch. The car jerks forward into a stall, and I shriek. I'm not thinking straight.

When the engine is finally quiet, I rest my head against the steering wheel. It's all I can do.

I soak up the silence for a few moments. A car door closes, but I can't be bothered to look up.

I take a deep breath. Another. Another.

Steady. Come back to earth, Jenessa.

I hear feet crunching on gravel. Another car door opens.

Dmitri's voice reaches me from a million miles away.

"Looks like they've been waiting for him." He's holding my door open, leaning on the frame. I don't lift my head. Instead, I stare at his leg. His boot. The little crack in the sole right where it connects with the toe. The dust around the stitching.

The night air cools my skin. I wait for my breathing to return to normal.

"I don't know how," he continues, "but I saw them there, lying in wait. I'm sure they've been wanting to make a bust for quite some time."

I look up at his face.

He smiles at me. "Thought I'd let them catch the badass tonight."

I rub my hands over my face. I run my hands through my hair and sit back in my seat. I stare up at the roof. Let out a long breath.

Finally I turn to look at him. "Yeah?" I say. I give him a weak smile. "Who says they caught the right one?"

He grins and stoops to kiss me.

I want to cry. I want to laugh.

I want to live.

Acknowledgments

My thanks to Beth Gracia, my track-racing insurance agent (!), who was a great source of information in writing this book.

Alex Van Tol has been writing for as long as she can remember. A freelance writer, she is the author of *Knifepoint*, *Viral* and *Gravity Check*, all from Orca Book Publishers. Alex lives in Victoria, British Columbia, and dreams of Bora Bora.

orca soundings

For more information on all the books
in the Orca Soundings series, please visit
www.orcabook.com.